we L.I.G.I.T:

We Let Intelligence Guide our Intentions and Thoughts

Kriss Kicks and Mel

Martha Joseph Watts

we L.I.G.I.T: Kriss Kicks and Mel
We Let Intelligence Guide our Intentions and Thoughts
Story one
Copyright © by Martha Joseph Watts
ISBN: 979-8-9857466-1-7
Rev. Date 03/02/2022

This short story is a work of fiction. The places, events, names, and incidents are fictitious and are the product of the author's imagination. Any resemblance to businesses or actual persons living or dead is entirely unintentional.

To order additional copies of this short story, contact:
Buddinwriters at 407 430 8055 or
E-mail: drwatts@buddinwriters.com

Martha Joseph Watts, Ed.D
Author, Instructor, Educational Consultant

Printed in the Unites States of America

Dedication

To middle grade boys and girls everywhere.
To black middle grade boys and girls
everywhere; Be authentic. Do not be defined
by people's expectations or preconceived
perceptions of you.
Be real. Show off your brilliance.

To Quani, Eli, Anna, and Neema
To Cameron and Bryan

Acknowledgements

Special thanks to my Full Sail professor and classmates for inspiring and guiding this story.
Thanks to my team of dedicated readers, my editor, my family, and friends for their consistent belief and patience with me during those creative moments.
Thanks to God Almighty for sustaining my creative thirst.

Kriss Kicks and Mel

"Mel, will you be my date for spring dance?"

Ever since I heard the date for our spring dance, I promised to be the first to ask Mel. Over the weekend, I practiced my top two searches to perfection.

"Melané Jean, please, be my spring dance date."

I bubbled with excitement at the thought of just looking at her to ask. I glanced at my phone, peeped at her glowing eyes, and the same feeling resurfaced. A cool, refreshing sensation engulfed my body much the same as what cold drinks evoked at half-time.

I examined myself in the mirror. Each curl stood exactly how I wanted, and my garbs complimented each other down to my new shoes. Satisfied, I picked up my old ivory-colored sneakers, thanked them for their service, and stuffed them into a large, brown paper bag. I checked the mirror one last time, cracked my bedroom door open, and scoured the hallway for mom's lurking eyes. Then, with one look down at my new shoes, I trotted down the wooden stairs. I grabbed my bag pack and bolted for the back door where our trashcan stayed.

Dang it! Dad. He had already left.

The large, green trashcan stood on the cluttered sidewalk. My confidence dropped. Vexed at my dad's commitment, I made a sucking noise through my teeth as I vowed to give my old sneakers a decent burial.

If dad had already left, then mom might be up early, although her job at the public library didn't start until ten. A slight fog served as camouflage. Still uneasy, I surveyed the neighboring apartment porches and windows for any early-morning wandering eyes. The cool December morning breeze tickled my face, and with each calculated step, my toes searched for comfort. I pranced three units down towards the curb of one of my dog-walking customers, Mr. Smith.

Still looking for suspicious gazes, I hastened my steps. The irritation at my heels increased, but I persisted and made it in time. I loomed towards Mr. Smith's trash can, and like a respectful pall bearer, deposited my brown paper bag underneath a pile of old newspapers. Relieved, I looked down in admiration at my new kicks. They added to my stature. I felt proud.

Noise from the approaching school bus jolted me back to reality.

"Hey, Jehmel, your ole-man night shift just done." That was Matthew, the most annoying kid on my bus.

"Ha ha," joked Karl, "did you have to change diapers?"

"Good morning, Mr. Alfred," I said, ignoring

the boys' insults.

I wiggled my way to the back of the bus and plopped in the middle seat.
Jasmine, the girl to my right, noticed my new shoes and started the chatter that served as the morning's topic. "Wow, J," she leaned over, touching my shoes. "Your kicks look kriss."

"Where you geh those?" Jake asked.

"Somebody len em to him. He can' afford that brand," Leon added before I could respond to Jake.

"Postman Jules ain't geh no money to waste on latest brand," Joel added.

Laughter erupted through the entire bus, and all eyes latched on me. Kids leaned halfway over their seats to look at my red, white, and blue sneakers.

"Sit down! Sit down!" Mr. Alfred yelled.

They lagged, but everyone retreated to their seats.

I cleared my throat. "Hey, hold up! So, y'all think, I be walking dogs and scooping poop for free?"

The hydraulic sound of the stopping bus interrupted and ended my speech moment. Neither my parents nor teachers would have recognized this Jehmel speech. I practically, grew up on my mom's job. It served as an unofficial aftercare during my elementary school years. On those afternoons, I saturated myself in books while my friends most likely did the same in video games. Each week, I looked forward to learning new things. Those days paid off. But navigating middle school as a bright boy from my neighborhood came with challenges. Over time, I developed the skills of juggling both my speech and swag.

I hopped off the bus behind three dozen students. Apart from ensuring that no one trampled on my new shoes, I pondered on how to find the perfect time to be the first to ask Mel to be my spring dance date. The thought nagged me.

Car riders usually came to school earlier than bus riders, so Mel would already be at school. I stepped into the halls hoping that I would run into Mel before the bell. As more students converged in the halls, mixed smells greeted my nostrils. Colognes, lotions, hair spray, cigarette, and even pet smells. Girls shrieked as they approached their friends, and boys dapped each other.

All I wanted was a glimpse of Mel. I blushed at the thought of her name.

"Hey J," a familiar voice called. Before even turning, my stomach sank a notch. Her dark eyes beamed beneath her French-braided hair adorned with sleek edges. Her smile revealed her three dimples. I melted in the moment.

"Hi, Jehmel," her friend, Sue, muttered. The girls with arms locked at the elbows, smiled, and waltzed off. My heart fluttered.

I managed to shelter my new shoes from flipflop-trotting kids, but I missed an opportunity to ask Mel. Her lingering melodic voice dissolved the sound of the school bell, but the rush of students headed in different directions alerted me. I headed to class, but my mind boggled over my missed opportunity. At least, I still had lunch to strategize.

The loudest bell brought an end to the longest part of my day. I dashed out of the classroom, hoping to earn an early spot on the lunch line. Those of us who ate at school entered the cafeteria later. That sucked. Mel brought her own lunch, so she scored early sitting space with friends.

My head throbbed, thinking up one-hundred-and-one ways to get to Mel. Skip lunch? Cut the line? Bribe a seventh grader for a fair exchange in school-currency? These thoughts took turns in my swirling brain, then wore out. I still stood in the same place in line.

Any of these options risked an encounter with gruff Officer Jones, the school resource, or police officer. He planted his broad, tall body in the doorway on guard for almost any illegal entry. I'd had my run-ins with him before. Today? Too sacred to mess up.

"Dem kicks look on," a random student said.

"Nuff sweat to geh em," I replied.

The growl from my stomach nudged me, but food would have to wait. I eased my way into the cafeteria. As usual, the noise, an annoying combination of teenagers greeting, dissing, cheering, laughing, or plain old screaming, bombarded the space much like a stadium during a home game. Luckily, blocking out noise is a teen-talent. I positioned myself on the right of the entrance and conducted a methodical survey of a section of the dining area while standing clear of the flipflop-wearing kids who lacked respect for those of us with kriss kicks.

There she sat. On the third row of tables. Smiling and chatting with her friends. I spotted Kam at the crowded table. Smart dude, but I detested him. Not in a beefing way. We solved difficult math problems together in algebra class, and we played on the school's varsity basketball team. Everything changed when I walked in on his dirty talk to Mel and her friends.

"You girls must stay clear of boys from the hood," he had said.

I never perceived him the same way since. I dismissed the negative thoughts. I eyed Mel, and the impact of her smile came flying over the heads of the clamoring students.

My left hand clutched the waistline of my pants, and the other hand automatically latched on to the handle of my backpack. I had to remember my walk. Parted legs. No bending of the feet. Middle schoolers frowned on shoes creased on the front over the toes, and the only way to maintain that smooth kris look was to walk as if there was an urgent need for the bathroom.

"Penguin, what happened? You pooped your pants or bought the wrong size?" Mick, the tallest white boy in my English class, asked. He knew how to press my buttons.

"Mind your frigging busi–" Before I completed my sentence, the hulk of our school plodded on my foot.

Infuriated, I threw my arms mid-air and heaved my five-feet, five-inch self as close to his face as possible. Before my hands dropped, a set of strong hands hijacked them from the back.

Officer Jones gave me a 180-degree spin. "Jehmel, look at me, boy. What are you doing?"

"Nothing," I responded with my head barely

meeting his gaze.

"What do you mean, nothing?" Officer Jones continued, "You violated the personal space policy.
You've lost your freedom. I will walk you to lunch."

I followed Officer Jones like a naughty kindergartener on the way to time out. My eyes met the large brown print the hulk's flipflop left on my brand-new, hard-earned shoe. Rage moved within, but I still had Mel to impress. Focused on cooling down, I clinched my teeth until my temple hurt, but that helped.

Going through the lunch-line with an adult makes a difference. Quick. Humiliating sometimes, but today I welcomed it as a secret service escort for me and my shoes.

I wanted the rice and peas with teriyaki chicken, but this wasn't a day to engage in messy eating.

"One slice of cheese pizza, please?" I asked.

Ms. Marti looked up but stopped short of asking if I was ill today. She was one of those café workers who had eyes like our mama. She kept us straight and gave us extra servings if we asked properly.

"Thank you, ma'am," I said, with a new sense of politeness. Confident, that I had cooled down, Officer Jones left. I balanced my slice of pizza and the small three-ounce juice on my cardboard tray. Without any thought, I headed in the direction of Mel and her friends, who seemed to be in the middle of a circus fair.

I normalized my walk to suit a decent "A" brown boy walk and approached the group. No available seats near Mel. I advanced anyway.

One girl commented as I passed a table, "Those are cool shoes."

This was no time for distraction. I kept strutting.

I scrutinized Mel as she savored a cherry ice-cream. The sight empowered my walk. As I got closer, my stomach produced a sensation that erased hunger and fear. The feeling created a blend of happiness and excitement that rushed my entire body. I made it close enough to stand behind her.

"Mel, behind you," her friend warned. My best camera smile waited to capture those black-diamond eyes. She spun around, and I admired her odd-dimpled smile, and relished my short-lived moment. The cherry ice-cream she had just licked dislodged from the security of its cone and landed on the white part of my brand-new shoes.

"WOOOOOOOOOOOE," came a sea of voices drowning anything that came from her mouth.

I refocused my attention to Mel in time to

notice her eyes transformed to reflect regret mixed with empathy.

"I am so sorry," she mouthed in slow motion.

PING, PING, PING.

Like spectators after a victory game, students dashed out the cafeteria, and I stood in between awe and despair. Neither of them winning.

Mel reached into her bag and retrieved a pouch. It read: *Athletic Shoe Cleaner*.

"Sorry," she said in her tender and calming voice while handing me the kit. In a caring, yet hurried whisper she continued, "I'll see you later. I can't be late to class."

As she swung her head to leave, I said, "Mel, will you be my spring date," instead of saying thank you.

She released the sweetest smile, and a

wink before joining the departing crowd. I watched her hair bounce to the rhythm of her model-like gait as she camouflaged with the dissipating mob.

I had a new task, but I had company—the refreshing feeling and new hope.

I hopscotched over spilled grapes and occasional puddles of applesauce towards the paper towel rack. I whipped off the melted slush and reminisced with regret on this morning's burial ceremony. My old shoes were in better shape. But at least I can clean these later.

VIBBBBBB! I snatched my phone and glanced.

MEL: "Hey J. I am excited about what we will wear."

My palms moistened, I screamed, and leaped for the door. I headed to algebra class. Late, but I'll see her one more time.

VIBBBBB! Another text?

MOM: The image of a brown paper bag in the middle of my bed with a message—Delivery from Mr. Smith.

Sucks. But that can wait.

END

About the author

Dr. Martha Joseph Watts, a native of the Caribbean Island of Dominica, resides in Florida where she continues to serve as an educator. She holds a Master of Fine Arts in Creative Writing with Full Sail university. Among her self-published works are educational resources and children's fiction chapter books. *Kriss Kicks and Mel* starts her latest series for middle grade readers.